Alphabet~~X~~BETTER

story by Dan Bar-el

illustrations by Graham Ross

ORCA BOOK PUBLISHERS

For every preschool teacher, kindergarten teacher and early childhood educator—passing on the gift of language one letter at a time. And a special thanks to David for being a good friend.
—Dan Bar-el

A,B,C,D, who do I thank but thee
A—it be Heather, my sister who shines
B—it be Ian, who's mighty fine
My love to you both
—Graham Ross

If you search (and search and search), you will find a letter of the alphabet hidden in the picture on each page of this book, *a* on the A page, *b* on the B page and so on. For the answer key, go to *Alphabetter* at www.orcabook.com. Good luck finding them all!

Text copyright © 2006 Dan Bar-el   Illustrations copyright © 2006 Graham Ross

Library and Archives Canada Cataloguing in Publication

Bar-el, Dan

Alphabetter / story by Dan Bar-el; illustrations by Graham Ross.

"Bet" in the title word, Alphabet, crossed out and replaced with "Better".

ISBN 10: 1-55143-439-3

ISBN 13: 978-1-55143-439-1

1. English language--Alphabet--Juvenile literature. 2. Alphabet books.

I. Ross, Graham, 1962- II. Title.

PE1155.B36 2006   j421'.1   C2006-901773-5

First published in the United States 2006

Library of Congress Control Number: 2006924161

Summary: In this offbeat alphabet book, children find themselves with the wrong objects for the tasks at hand until they find a way to help each other out.

Orca Book Publishers gratefully acknowledges the support for its publishing programs provided by the following agencies: the government of Canada through the Book Publishing Industry Development Program, the Canada Council for the Arts, the government of British Columbia and the British Columbia Arts Council.

Interior and cover artwork created using acrylics and collage.   Scanning: Island Graphics, Victoria, British Columbia.   Design and typesetting by Lynn O'Rourke.

Orca Book Publishers
PO Box 5626, Stn. B
Victoria, BC Canada
V8R 6S4

Orca Book Publishers
PO Box 468
Custer, WA USA
98240-0468

Printed and bound in Hong Kong   09 08 07 • 5 4 3 2

* ZAMBONI and the configuration of the ZAMBONI ice resurfacing machine are registered in the U.S. Patent and Trademark Office as the trademarks of Frank J. Zamboni & Co., Inc.

Alberto had an alligator,

but he didn't have a bathing suit.

Benoît had a bathing suit,

but he didn't have a clarinet.

Cara had a clarinet,

but she didn't have a doggy bone.

Dinah had a doggy bone,

but she didn't have an egg.

Edward had an egg,

but he didn't have a football.

Frieda had a football,

but she didn't have a goldfish.

Gwendolyn had a goldfish,

but she didn't have a hammer.

H

Hector had a hammer,

but he didn't have an ice cream.

Ina had an ice cream,

but she didn't have a jewel.

J

Joo Pyo had a jewel,

but she didn't have a kite.

K

Kalil had a kite,

but he didn't have a letter.

Louise had a letter,

but she didn't have a marshmallow.

Mateo had a marshmallow,

but he didn't have a necktie.

N Noah had a necktie,

but he didn't have an oar.

Orion had an oar,

but he didn't have a paintbrush.

P

Parker had a paintbrush,

but she didn't have a quail.

Quinn had a quail,

but she didn't have a rag doll.

Rohin had a rag doll,

AUDITIONS
TODAY:
CINDERFELLER

but he didn't have a slipper.

Sasha had a slipper,

but he didn't have a toy train.

Talia had a toy train,

but she didn't have an umbrella.

U

Umar had an umbrella,

but she didn't have a vase.

Vladimir had a vase,

but he didn't have a water ski.

Wallace had a water ski,

but he didn't have a xylophone.

Xena had a xylophone,

but she didn't have a yoga mat.

Yanni had a yoga mat,

but he didn't have a Zamboni.*

*Zamboni ® ice resurfacer

Zara had a Zamboni,*

*Zamboni ® ice resurfacer

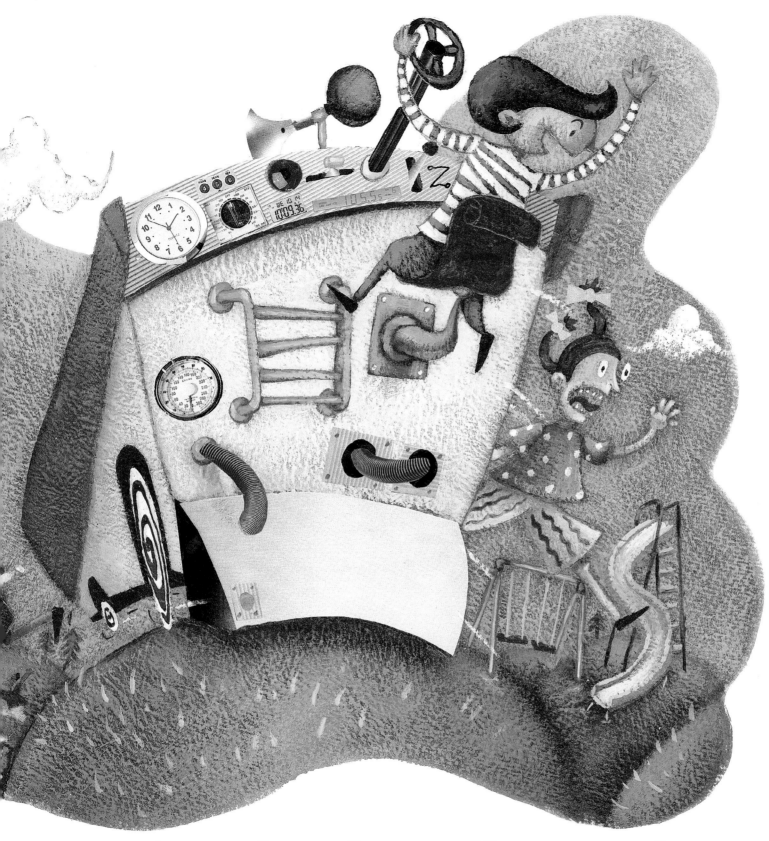

but what she really wanted was a friend.

So...

Zara gave the Zamboni* to Yanni,

and Yanni gave the yoga mat to Xena,

and Xena gave the xylophone to Wallace,

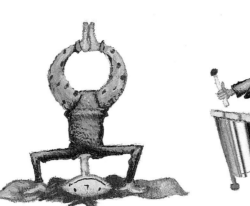

and Wallace gave the water ski to Vladimir,

and Rohin gave the rag doll to Quinn,

and Parker gave the paintbrush to Orion,

and Quinn gave the quail to Parker,

and Orion gave the oar to Noah,

and Joo Pyo gave
the jewel to Ina,

and Hector gave the hammer to Gwendolyn,

and Frieda gave the football to Edward,

and Ina gave the ice cream to Hector,

and Gwendolyn gave
the goldfish to Frieda,

*Zamboni ® ice resurfacer

and Vladimir gave the vase to Umar

and Umar gave the umbrella to Talia,

and Talia gave the toy train to Sasha,

and Sasha gave the slipper to Rohin,

and Noah gave the
necktie to Mateo,

and Mateo gave the marshmallow to Louise,

and Louise gave the letter to Kalil,

and Kalil gave the kite to Joo Pyo,

and Dinah gave the
doggy bone to Cara,

and Benoît gave the bathing suit
to Alberto,

and Edward gave the egg to Dinah,

and Cara gave the clarinet to Benoît,

and Alberto gave the alligator to the zoo.

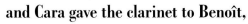

Then he phoned Zara and invited her over for a swim.